FESTIVALS OF THE WORLD

EGYPT

mc Marshall Cavendish
Benchmark
New York

This edition first published in 2011 in
the United States of America by
Marshall Cavendish Benchmark.

Marshall Cavendish Benchmark
99 White Plains Road
Tarrytown, NY 10591
Website: www.marshallcavendish.us

© Marshall Cavendish International (Asia)
Pte Ltd 2011
Originated and designed by Marshall Cavendish
International (Asia) Pte Ltd
A member of Times Publishing Limited
Times Centre, 1 New Industrial Road
Singapore 536196

Written by: Elizabeth Berg
Edited by: Crystal Chan
Designed by: Lock Hong Liang/Steven Tan
Picture research: Thomas Khoo
Library of Congress Cataloging-in-Publication
Data

Berg, Elizabeth.
Egypt / by Elizabeth Berg.
p. cm. -- (Festivals of the world)
Includes bibliographical references and index.
Summary: "This book explores the exciting culture
and many festivals that are celebrated in Egypt"--
Provided by publisher.
ISBN 978-1-60870-097-4
1. Festivals--Egypt--Juvenile literature. 2. Egypt--
Social life and customs--Juvenile literature. I. Title.
GT4888.A2.B47 2011
394.260962--dc22
2010000215
ISBN 978-1-60870-097-4

Printed in Malaysia

1 3 6 5 4 2

Contents

It's Festival Time . . .

Egypt is an ancient civilization with a very rich culture. Some festivals in Egypt can be traced back to the time of the pharaohs. For thousands of years, Egyptians have enjoyed boating on the Nile or the "Smelling the Breeze" festival. Put on some new clothes and come join the adventure. It's festival time in Egypt!

Where's Egypt?

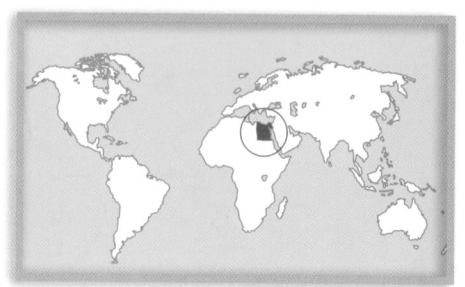

Egypt is located in the northeast corner of Africa. Most of Egypt is covered by the Western Desert, part of the Sahara. The Nile River cuts through Egypt, flowing from its source in tropical Africa to the Mediterranean Sea. For thousands of years, the yearly flooding of the Nile made the land on its banks very fertile. In ancient times, the Nile River made Egypt an important trading center and a very rich country.

Who Are the Egyptians?

Ancient Egypt is one of the oldest civilizations in the world. Many modern cultures have their roots in ancient Egypt. The **pharaohs** ruled Egypt for many thousands of years until they were conquered by invaders. Egypt then became a Christian nation. Much later, **Islam** swept over the region. Today most Egyptians are Muslim, but there are also some that practice Christianity who are called **Coptic Christians**, or Copts.

✳ An Egyptian girl. Modern Egyptians are a mixture of many different peoples.

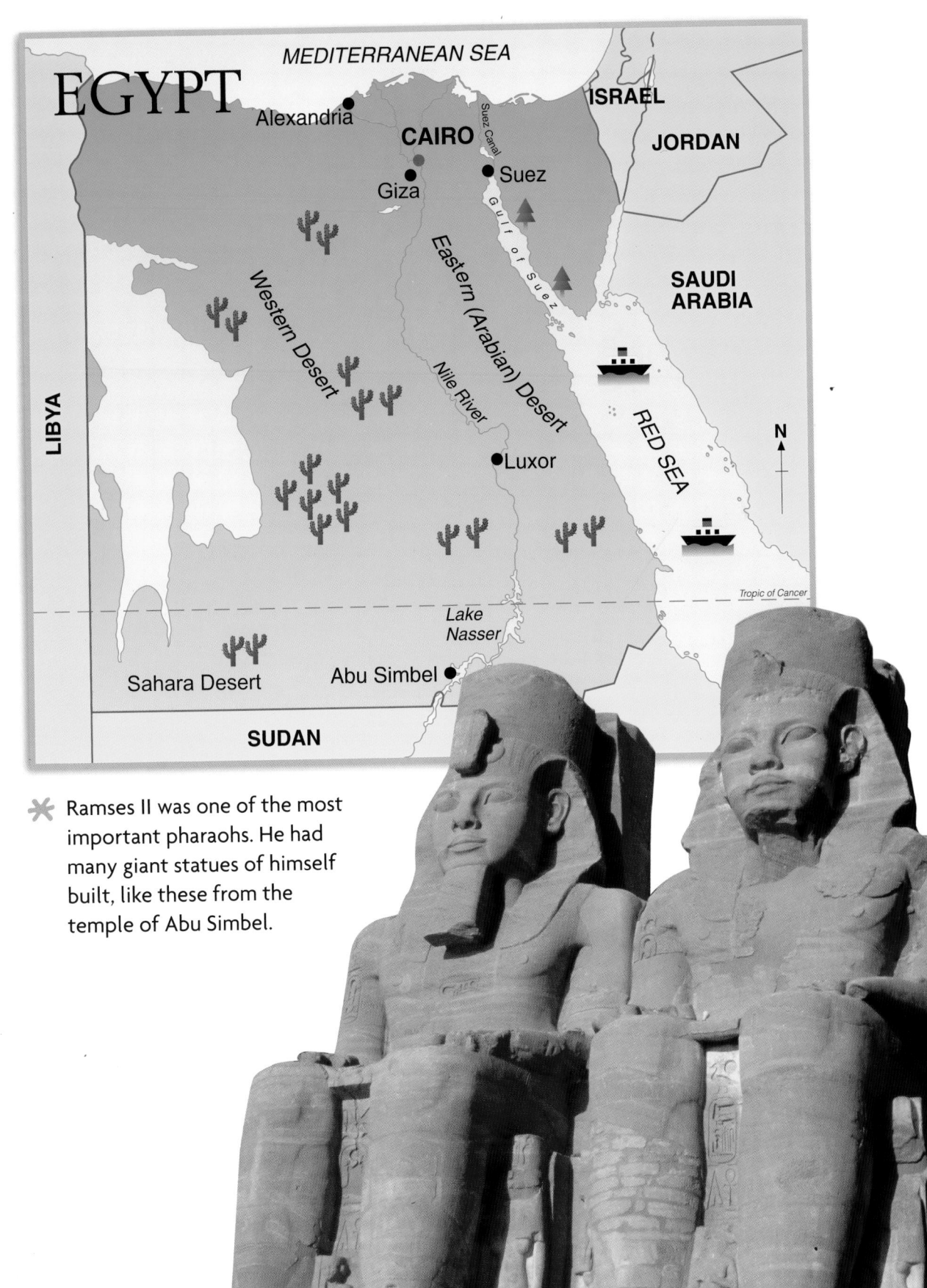

MEDITERRANEAN SEA

EGYPT

Alexandria

CAIRO

ISRAEL

JORDAN

Suez Canal

Suez

Giza

Eastern (Arabian) Desert

Gulf of Suez

SAUDI ARABIA

Western Desert

Nile River

LIBYA

Luxor

RED SEA

N

Tropic of Cancer

Lake Nasser

Sahara Desert

Abu Simbel

SUDAN

* Ramses II was one of the most important pharaohs. He had many giant statues of himself built, like these from the temple of Abu Simbel.

What Are the Festivals?

We're going to a mawlid! Put on your party hat and join us!

There are three calendars in Egypt. The Islamic calendar is **lunar** and follows the phases of the moon. Muslim holidays move back eleven days each year, so they slowly move through the seasons. The Copts follow another calendar. This one is based on the calendar invented by the ancient Egyptians. Farmers in Egypt still follow it to find out when to plant and harvest crops. For most day-to-day things, Egyptians follow the widely used Gregorian calendar.

MUSLIM HOLIDAYS

* **Muharram**—This festival celebrates the Muslim New Year and Prophet Muhammad's flight from Mecca to Medina.

* **Mawlid an-Nabi**—Commemorates Prophet Muhammad's birthday.

* **Ramadan**—A month when Muslims fast during the daylight hours and have their meals when night falls. It is a time of worship and contemplation. People also work to strengthen their family and community ties.

- **Id al-Fitr**—The end of the fasting month when children dress in new clothes and celebrate with friends and family.
- **Id al-Adha**—An important Islamic festival in remembrance of Ibrahim's sacrifice. People also go on the hajj, or pilgrimage, to Mecca during this time.

SPRING

- **Easter**—On this day, Christians celebrate Jesus Christ's return to life. Many people take palm branches home from church and weave them into crosses.
- **Sham al-Nasim**—The day after Easter Sunday, Sham al-Nasim marks the beginning of spring. The people enjoy picnic lunches in the park and boating on the Nile.
- **Annunciation**—An important Coptic feast day.

SUMMER

- **National Day**—This day celebrates the revolution when King Farouk I was overthrown and Egypt became a republic.
- **Feast of the Virgin Mary**—Celebrates Mary, one of the most popular Christian saints.
- **Nile Festivals**—The Nile River has always been the center of Egyptian festivities and continues to play a role in festivals held throughout the summer.

AUTUMN

- **Armed Forces Day**—The celebration of the Egyptian army's crossing into Sinai in 1973.

WINTER

- **Christmas**—Celebrated on January 7 in Egypt, Christians attend a church service the night before Christmas and then return home to enjoy a midnight feast with their families. Gifts are exchanged on Christmas Day.
- **Epiphany**—The day when Christians celebrate the baptism of Jesus Christ.

Let's make some music, Egyptian-style!

Ramadan

Ramadan is a time when Muslims celebrate the Prophet Muhammad, the founder of Islam, and Islam's holy book—the **Qur'an**. It is not really a festival. Rather, it is a holy month in which people fast, much like the Catholic Lent. Ramadan is also a time to strengthen one's faith and practice self-control. For an entire month, Muslims fast from sunrise to sundown. They do not eat or drink. For some, even licking a stamp is forbidden. People wake up very early in the morning, so they can eat a good meal called *sohour* [SO-hore] before the Sun comes up. As soon as it is light outside, lanterns hung all around Egyptian cities are put out, and no one may eat or drink anything until the lanterns are lit again at dusk. After night falls, Muslims eat a big meal called *iftar* [EEF-tar], which means breakfast, because they are breaking their fast.

✳ Left: The iftar meal usually begins with a drink of water or a date. After a prayer, people enjoy the rest of the meal.

✳ Opposite: Ramadan lanterns brighten a Cairo street.

Breaking the Fast

The celebration starts every night with the iftar meal. Long into the night, Muslims continue feasting and talking with friends and family, listening to Arabic music and Islamic readings on the radio. Some go to the mosque together to pray. Restaurants and shops are open late, and the streets are full of people.

✳ During Ramadan, Muslims spend a lot of time reading the Qur'an and praying at mosques.

✳ Dates are usually eaten when breaking the fast and are bought at outdoor markets before Ramadan.

Muhammad's Teachings

One of the laws set down in the Qur'an is that Muslims should fast during the month of Ramadan. The Qur'an not only tells Muslims about God, but it tells them about how they should live. Muslims believe that the Prophet Muhammad received the Qur'an from the Angel Gabriel while meditating in a cave. Muhammad could not read or write, but he memorized the entire Qur'an so he could tell the people what God said. Later his followers wrote down the Qur'an. Muhammad went out and told the people of Mecca that there was only one god, called **Allah**, which means the God. The religion he preached is called Islam, which means submission. Today there are communities of Muslims living on every continent.

> **THINK ABOUT THIS**
>
> Muslims believe in the same prophets as Christians do. In addition, they believe that the last and most important prophet was Muhammad. They call Christians and Jews "the people of the Book" because, like Muslims, they follow the Bible.

Id al-Fitr

In the past, on the evening of the twenty-ninth day of Ramadan, the chief judge would be escorted by a great procession to Moqattam Hill to look for the new moon. If he was able to see the moon, the announcement was made that the fasting month had ended. If he could not see it, Ramadan would continue for another day. Today an observatory is used to look for the new moon. An announcement is made when the moon is sighted. If it is a cloudy night, reports may be sent from other Muslim countries to let people know that the fasting month is over. Then people know that the next day will be Id al-Fitr, and their fast is finished.

✳ Women usually get together to prepare special foods for Id. These women are making *kahk*, a traditional pastry served for Id.

✳ Everyone goes to special Id prayers. These are often held outside in parks or in city squares.

Dressing Up

✳ Muhammad Ali Mosque in Cairo lit up for the holidays.

Before Id comes, people paint and decorate their house, buy gifts, and send greeting cards to neighbors, friends, and relatives. On the day of the festival, they wake up early and put on their best clothes. Many children get new clothes for Id. Then all the men and boys go to the mosque to pray. Women and girls either go to the mosque or stay at home to prepare a big feast.

✳ Families go out to the park or sailing on the Nile for Id.

A Day to Have Fun

After going to the mosque to pray, Muslims go out to the park or go sailing on the Nile. All around you can hear people greeting each other with the words "*Id Mubarak*" [EED moo-BAH-rak], which means happy Id. It is also a good time for family reunions and visiting friends. People who live far away from their family always try to come home for the holiday. It is a time to resolve any quarrels and to spend time with friends and family. Muslims also think about others at this time of year. If they can afford it, many people give money at the mosque. This money is given to the poor of the community, so that they can also take part in the Id festivities.

THINK ABOUT THIS

There are really only two important festivals for Muslims: Id al-Fitr and Id al-Adha. That is because Muslims are supposed to practice their faith every day, not just a few days of the year.

✳ Opposite: Children dressed up in their new clothes for the holiday.

Id al-Adha

Another important Islamic festival is Id al-Adha, which means Feast of the Sacrifice. The holiday celebrates the biblical story of a man named Abraham, also known as Ibrahim by Muslims. According to the story, God told Ibrahim to go to the mountain and sacrifice his son. Ibrahim obeyed God's command. Before he cut the boy's throat, though, he covered his eyes. When he uncovered them, he found that he had sacrificed a sheep instead. His son was alive.

Important Sacrifices

Id al-Adha is also a time for celebration.

Celebrating Id al-Adha reminds people that, like Ibrahim, they must be willing to make sacrifices for God. To show their willingness to sacrifice, many Muslims buy an animal and kill it. In the days before the festival, the streets of Cairo are filled with sheep. After the sheep are sacrificed, the owners give away one-third of the meat to friends, one-third to family, and one-third to the poor. Then everyone celebrates the holiday with a big feast.

Take a Holy Trip

Id al-Adha is also the time of year when Muslims fulfill an important obligation. Every Muslim who is able to must visit Mecca. This trip is called the *hajj* [HAHDGE]. People go on the hajj during Id al-Adha. They visit the *Ka'ba* [kah-AH-bah], a square black building that is a sacred shrine. Other rituals also celebrate important moments in Ibrahim's life. At hajj time, millions of Muslims from all over the world come together to worship Allah. It is one of the most important events in a Muslim's life.

* According to Muslim tradition, the Ka'ba was built by Ibrahim. Here the courtyard of the mosque at Mecca is filled with pilgrims, who walk around the Ka'ba three times.

* One Egyptian tradition is to paint a mural on the wall of your home after you have been on the hajj.

Mawlid an-Nabi

Let's go to El-Hussein Square in Cairo. It's the eleventh day of the month of Rabi al-Awwal, the day when Muslims celebrate the birth of Muhammad. Big tents are set up all around the square. Colored lights are draped from the buildings, and the streets are aglow. Holy men recite the Qur'an and poems in praise of the Prophet. Inside the tents, delicious food is served. Soon a great procession will begin, when musicians from the army lead all the religious groups, carrying their banners and singing praises to the Prophet, back to El-Hussein Square. This is Mawlid an-Nabi, the Birthday of the Prophet.

* A Sufi dancer shows off his skill. At a mawlid, music can be heard everywhere, and there are special performances all around.

What Happens at a Mawlid?

Mawlid [MOW-lid] means birth. It is a celebration of the birthday of an important religious person. A few days before, big tents are put up, and the area is decorated with banners and lights. On the day of the mawlid, there is a big **zaffa** [ZAH-fah] procession with much music and celebration. The best part may be the evening entertainment. Markets are set up where people can buy sweets, toys, clothes, and many other items. There are swings, merry-go-rounds, and puppet shows. There may also be a storyteller sharing exciting tales of adventure.

✳ Markets are set up at mawlids, and the area is decorated with banners and lights.

THINK ABOUT THIS

There are mawlids for everyone. Muslims celebrate important Islamic figures as well as holy men. Christians have one for the Virgin Mary and one for St. George. Jews celebrate the mawlid of Abu Hasira. There are over five thousand mawlids every year!

Christmas

Most Egyptians are Muslim but not all. There is also a very old group of Christians called the Copts. The group dates back to the time before Islam came to Egypt. The Copts have their own calendar and celebrate Christmas on January 7 instead of December 25. Copts fast during the day for several weeks before Christmas. After a midnight church service on January 6, they go home to break their fast, and children receive new clothes and gifts. Long ago, Muslims and Copts celebrated Christmas and many other holidays together. Today Copts celebrate many of their festivals at church.

✳ Christmas is a special occasion for the Copts in Egypt.

✳ Opposite: An important Coptic religious leader at the Christmas mass in Cairo.

Celebrating Nature

On the day after Easter Sunday, Egyptians celebrate a favorite festival called Sham al-Nasim. They get out of bed early in the morning and spend the day outside, enjoying nature. People take picnic lunches with them, and they go to the park or go boating on the Nile. They make sure to pack some salted fish, kidney beans, and some green onions. It is an old tradition to eat these foods on this special day. In fact, the tradition can be traced back to the ancient Egyptians. In ancient Egypt, people also celebrated the beginning of spring.

Sham al-Nasim

Sham al-Nasim means Smelling the Breeze. There is an old saying in Egypt that "he who sniffs the first spring zephyr [breeze] will have good health all year." Sham al-Nasim is a day set aside to breathe in the fresh spring air and enjoy a picnic. A hundred years ago, it was a harvest festival. At that time, it was the biggest festival in Egypt.

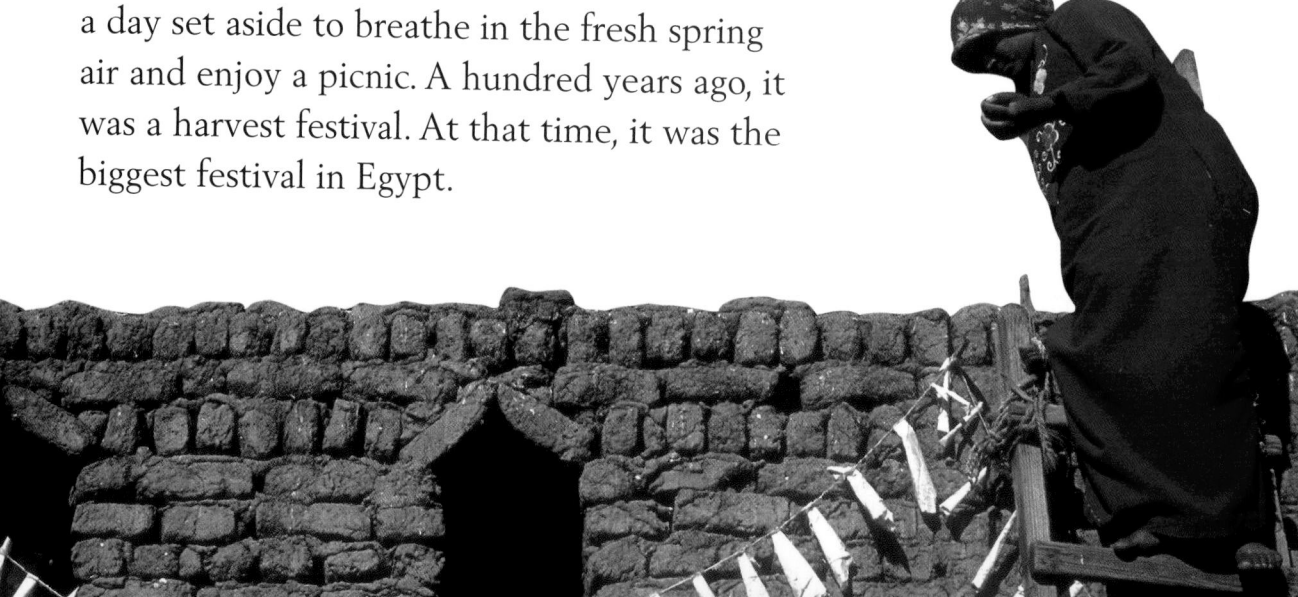

✱ A woman collects pigeon eggs. Eggs were a symbol of new life in ancient Egypt.

Have an Onion

Many people smell an onion first thing in the morning when they wake up on the day of Sham al-Nasim. They may also hang onions on the front door to protect their home. Egyptians believe that onions are very good for one's health and protect people from illness. The ancient Egyptians drew them in tomb paintings, believing onions could cure many illnesses.

✳ Egyptians enjoy the outdoors on Sham al-Nasim day.

✳ An ancient wall painting shows dancers and musicians. Festivals in ancient Egypt were celebrated with feasting, drinking, and dancing.

THINK ABOUT THIS

Do you celebrate any festivals when the seasons change? While some festivals only celebrate a season, others have a religious meaning, too. Can you think of any religious holidays that also celebrate a season?

✳ Nilometers were built in many temples to measure how much the Nile waters had risen during the flood season.

Celebrating the Nile

The Nile River has always been the center of Egyptian festivals. In ancient times, festivals often included a procession on the Nile. Today going out on the Nile is still part of many festivals. Every year in August, there is a festival just to celebrate the Nile. In ancient times, the Egyptians carried statues of the gods to the river. They also brought lamps on their boats, and sang and danced. They gave offerings to the river so that the river would rise and flood their farmland with fertile soil. All night long, they feasted and celebrated, each person drinking from the Nile waters. Today there is still a Nile festival, but it is much smaller.

In the 1960s, Egypt constructed the Aswan High Dam. The dam is so large that the Nile no longer floods every year. The Egyptians, however, still rely on the Nile for water and electricity.

✳ An ancient painting shows boatmen on the Nile.

✳ Opposite: People enjoy riding in a *felucca* [fuh-LUK-uh] down the Nile.

Things for You to Do

The ancient Egyptians used **hieroglyphics** to record ideas and sounds. Hieroglyphics is a form of writing in which pictures are used to represent different things. The ancient Egyptians used this type of writing for more than three thousand years!

How to Write in Hieroglyphics

Sound out the word you want to write, and find the hieroglyph that goes with each sound. Think about the sound and not the way the word is spelled in English. Now that you have the hieroglyphs, you just have to put them together. They can be written in any direction. Just make sure the animals and birds are facing toward the beginning of the word or sentence. Try writing your name or the word *book*.

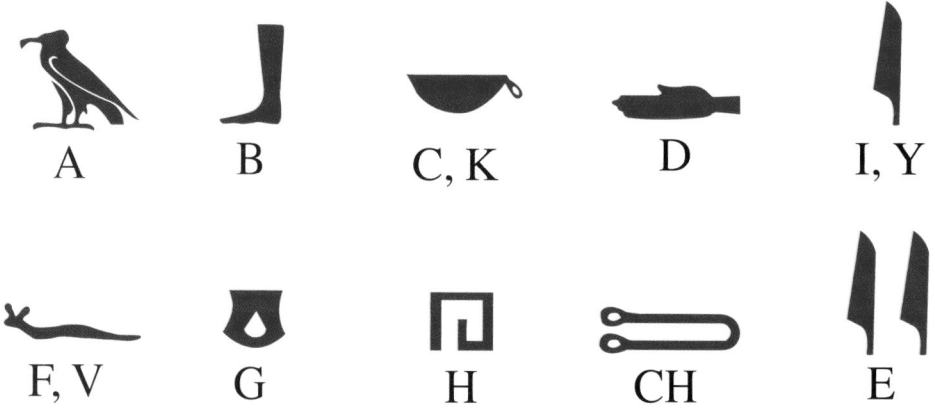

A B C, K D I, Y

F, V G H CH E

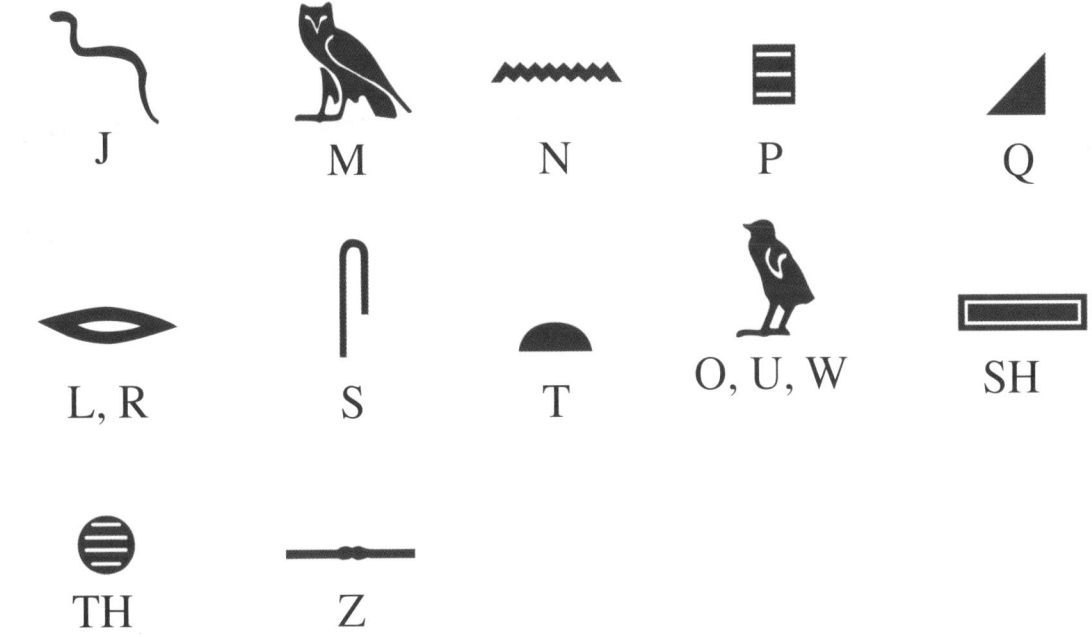

J   M   N   P   Q

L, R   S   T   O, U, W   SH

TH   Z

Make an Invitation

Now try to write an invitation to an Egyptian festival. Ancient Egyptians usually wrote important messages on a papyrus scroll. Papyrus is something like paper, but it is made from the papyrus plant, which grows along the Nile. Take a long piece of paper and write your invitation on it. Then roll up the paper and tie it with a ribbon.

FURTHER INFORMATION

Books: *Ancient Egypt.* George Hart (DK Children, 2008).
Egypt (Country Explorers). Tom Streissguth (Lerner Publications, 2007).
Egypt, the People. Arlene Moscovitch (Crabtree Publishing Company, 2008).
Life and Times in Ancient Egypt. Andrew Charman (Kingfisher, 2007).
Websites: http://guardians.net/egypt/kids/index.htm—Learn more about ancient Egyptian life and culture, with interesting facts and fun activities.
www.historyforkids.org/learn/egypt/—A good introduction to Egypt, covering a wide range of topics from history and people to food and clothing.

Make a Beaded Collar

The pharaohs used to wear wide collars set with precious stones. You can dress up just like the pharaohs with your own beaded collar!

1

3

2

4

5

6

8

7

You will need:
1. A ruler
2. Two 5-inch (12.5-cm) strips of velcro
3. A pencil
4. Scissors
5. Glue
6. Lace
7. Colored beads
8. A piece of felt

1 Draw a circle the size of your neck and then a wider one 5 inches (12.5 cm) larger than the first on the felt. Cut them out.

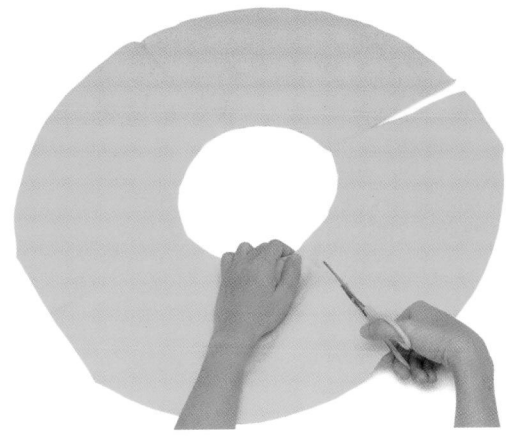

2 Cut out a section, a little less than 1/4 of the circle.

3 Glue pieces of velcro to the collar opening so that you will be able to fasten the collar closed.

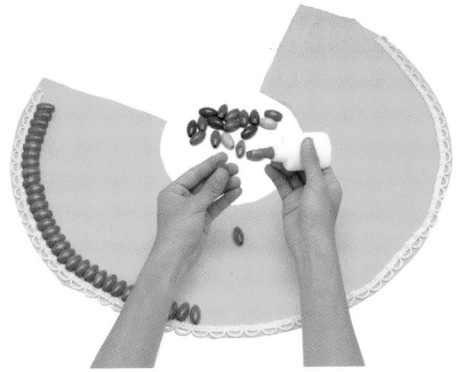

4 Use the glue to attach the beads in a pretty pattern. Attach the lace around the outer edge. Your collar is ready!

Make Grandma's Nut Cake

Egyptians make special sweet treats for Id al-Fitr. Here is one you could try at home with help from an adult.

You will need:

1. 1/2 cup (100 g) butter
2. 2 cups (450 g) sugar
3. 6 eggs
4. 3 cups (340 g) sifted flour
5. 3 teaspoons baking powder
6. 1 teaspoon ground cinnamon
7. 1/2 teaspoon salt
8. 2 cups (250 g) chopped nuts
9. 1 cup (240 ml) water
10. A pinch of fenugreek
11. A wooden spoon
12. A measuring cup for liquids
13. Measuring cups
14. A saucepan
15. Measuring spoons
16. Mixing bowls
17. A sifter
18. A baking pan
19. A pot holder

9 and 12

11

4   2   8   13

5   10   1

6

14   7

3 and 16   15

17, 18, and 19

1 Mix the butter and 1 1/2 cups (190 g) of sugar. Add the eggs one at a time, beating the mixture.

2 In another bowl, sift together the flour, baking powder, cinnamon, and salt. Pour the flour mixture into the egg mixture and mix well. Add the nuts.

3 Pour into a baking pan. It should be about 1 inch (2.5 cm) deep. Bake at 350°F (180°C) for 35 minutes. Ask an adult to help you with this part.

4 Combine the rest of the sugar, the water, and the fenugreek in a saucepan. Have an adult help you cook it over low heat, stirring constantly, until the sugar dissolves. Then boil it for three minutes. Pour the syrup over the cake.

Glossary

Allah	The Muslim name for God.
Coptic Christians	Members of the Egyptian Christian Church.
felucca	A traditional Egyptian boat that is used on the Nile.
hajj	A pilgrimage to Mecca by Muslims.
hieroglyphics	A special alphabet that was used in ancient Egypt.
iftar	The meal that breaks the fast during Ramadan.
Islam	A religion that follows the teachings of the Prophet Muhammad.
Ka'ba	A sacred shrine in Mecca.
lunar	Following the phases of the moon.
pharaohs	The rulers of ancient Egypt.
Qur'an	The Muslim holy book, sometimes spelled Koran.
sohour	The morning meal before fasting during Ramadan.
zaffa	A procession for a mawlid.

Index